Raccoon's Last Race

A TRADITIONAL ABENAKI STORY

AS TOLD BY **Joseph Bruchac & James Bruchac**

PICTURES BY **Jose Aruego & Ariane Dewey**

Dial Books for Young Readers • New York

Published by Dial Books for Young Readers
A division of Penguin Young Readers Group
345 Hudson Street
New York, New York 10014

Designed by Nancy R. Leo-Kelly
Text set in Elan
Manufactured in China on acid-free paper
10 9 8 7 6 5 4 3 2 1

Library of Congress Cataloging-in-Publication Data
Bruchac, Joseph, date.
Raccoon's last race : a traditional Abenaki story / Joseph Bruchac and James Bruchac ; pictures by Jose Aruego and Ariane Dewey.   p.   cm.
Summary: Tells the story of how Raccoon, the fastest animal on earth, loses his speed because he is boastful and breaks his promises.
ISBN 0-8037-2977-4
1. Abenaki Indians—Folklore. 2. Raccoons—Folklore. [1. Abenaki Indians—Folklore. 2. Indians of North America—Folklore. 3. Raccoons—Folklore.]
I. Bruchac, James. II. Aruego, Jose, ill. III. Dewey, Ariane, ill. IV. Title.   E99.A13.B79 2004   398.2'089'973—dc21   2003009104

The art for this book was prepared using pen-and-ink, gouache, and pastel.

To Wolfsong and his children —J.B. & J.B.

To Juan —J.A. & A.D.

Authors' Notes

There are probably no stories more popular among Abenaki children than those of Azban the Raccoon. There is a strong tradition of using stories rather than physical punishment as a means of disciplining children. How can a delightful story like this one fit in that tradition? Quite simply, Azban's misdeeds lead to his own downfall. What better way to illustrate the results of bad behavior? There's even a word in Abenaki, *Azebansoo,* which means "to act like Raccoon," or "to play a trick," that indicates how well-known Raccoon's behavior is. Azban is the kind of character called a Trickster, a human or animal who deliberately tries to deceive or cause trouble for others, but often ends up as the victim of his own actions. Two Abenaki elders, Maurice Dennis/Mdawelasis and Stephen Laurent/Atian Lolo, were the first to point me in the direction of the stories of Raccoon several decades ago. Stephen and Maurice both knew the ethnologist Frank Speck, whose "Penobscot Tales and Religious Beliefs," published in *The Journal of American Folklore* in 1935, contains a number of brief Azban tales. Some of the misfortunes that befall Azban (such as being flattened by a big rock and then seeking help) can also be found in the traditional tales of other American Indian nations. There's even a Pawnee story where Coyote is squashed and a Lakota tale where Iktomi ends up as flat as your hand. In all cases, the message of the Trickster tale remains the same: Be careful what you do. It may end up bringing trouble to you.

—Joseph Bruchac

From my earliest childhood, the Abenaki stories about Azban the Raccoon have been some of my favorites. Win or lose, Azban's Trickster ways, although quite comical, inspire lessons for young and old alike. I first heard this particular Azban story from my father. However, my own telling of it and other Azban tales was deeply influenced by the dramatic style and warm presence of our good friend Wolfsong, a great Abenaki storyteller whose voice and generosity of spirit are missed by all those who loved him and learned from him.

—James Bruchac

Long ago, Raccoon did not look the way he does today.

Back then, Azban the Raccoon had very long legs and was a fast runner. In fact, he was the fastest of all the animals. Because of this, he liked nothing better than to challenge the other animals to a race. With his long legs, he would always win.

He would race Bear. *Zip-zip!* He would beat Bear.

He would race Fox. *Zip-zip!* He would beat Fox.

He would race Rabbit. *Zip-zip!* He would beat Rabbit.

Azban the Raccoon also liked to taunt the other animals. While racing, he would turn his head back to look at his competitor and he would sing:

"Hee hee hee, look at me.
I am Azban, I am fast.
Look at you, ho ho ho!
You are very, very slow."

As you might imagine, this didn't please the other animals. After a while none would accept Azban's challenges. In fact, they even refused to speak to him because he was always trying to taunt them into racing again.

This didn't stop him. He began to play tricks on the other animals. He would hide in a tree, and when the animals walked by, he would jump down and frighten them. Because Azban was so fast, no one could ever catch him.

One day Azban noticed someone sitting on top of a tall hill. "Perhaps I can play a trick on that one. Perhaps I can challenge him to a race," Azban said. He quickly ran to the top of the hill.

But when he got there, he discovered that it was not an animal at all. It was a big rock. This did not stop Azban. He loved to talk, especially about himself. "Grandfather, are you a fast runner?" he asked. "I am Azban. I am the fastest of all the animals."

To Azban's surprise, Big Rock spoke back. In a deep voice it said, "No, Grandson, I do not travel. I just sit here."

"You should try it, Grandfather," Azban said.

"Grandson," Big Rock said, "I do not want to travel. I have been here for a long, long time. That is how it will always be."

Azban smiled. "Maybe not, Grandfather. I will help you."

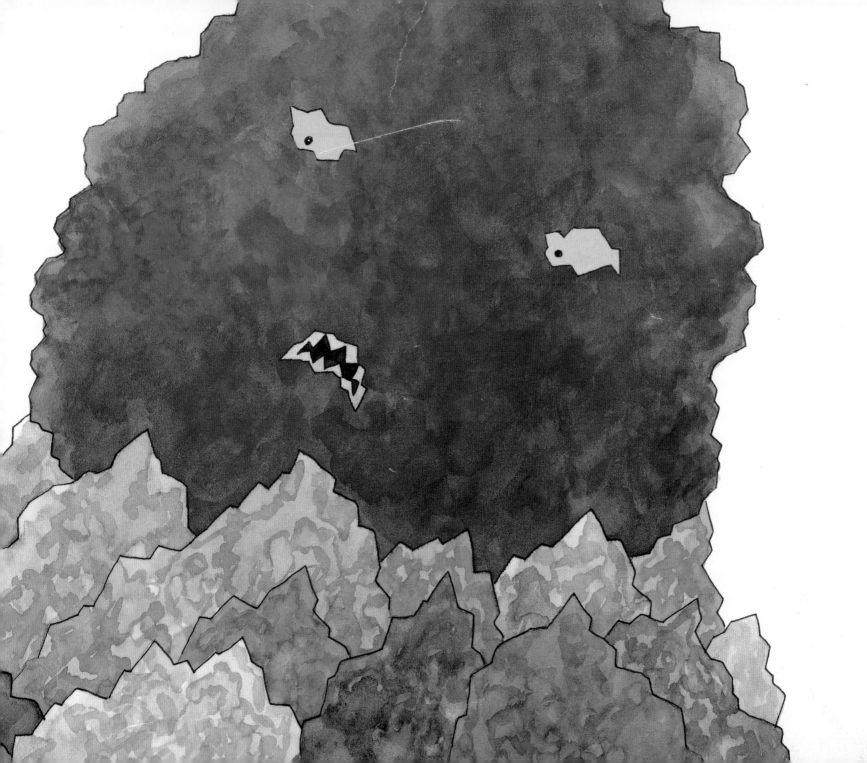

Then Azban got behind Big Rock and began to push and push. As he did so, the rock began to wobble back and forth. *Thump-thump, thump-thump.* Azban pushed harder and harder.

Ka-boom! The rock fell over on its side and began to roll. *Ka-boom!*
Ka-boom! Ka-boom! It rolled on down that hill.

"Aha, Grandfather," Azban shouted, "now you are traveling!"

As Big Rock rolled down the hill, Azban quickly caught up and ran alongside. "How do you like it?" he asked.

And Big Rock answered, *Ka-boom! Ka-boom! Ka-boom!*

Well, as that rock rolled down that hill, it naturally began to pick up speed. *Yippee,* thought Azban. *This rock is trying to challenge me to a race! I will show it a thing or two.*

Running as fast as he could, Azban the Raccoon flew past the rock that was rolling—*Ka-boom! Ka-boom!*—down the hill. He began to zigzag in front of Big Rock while turning around and taunting, "Ha ha! You are very slow, Grandfather. I, Azban, am very fast!"

But Azban turned his head to taunt that rock one time too many. Not looking where he was going, he tripped. *Ka-thunk!* He fell on the ground right in front of Big Rock.

Since the rock had never been traveling before, it didn't know how to stop. Instead it went *Ka-boom! Ka-boom! SPLAT! Ka-boom! Ka-boom! Ka-boom!* On and on the rock traveled, enjoying itself quite a bit.

And there lay Azban the Raccoon, rolled so flat and wide by the rock that he could not move his arms or legs or even his head. All he could move were his lips. "Help me. Somebody please help me," he said in a small, flattened-out voice. But no one seemed to hear Azban's cry for help. Or maybe, remembering all the tricks he had played, they did hear and pretended not to notice.

Bear skipped by, but didn't stop to help.

Fox trotted by, but didn't stop to help.

Rabbit—*ka-bunk, ka-bunk*—hopped right over him. Appeared not even to notice. Didn't stop to help.
One by one just about every animal in the forest passed Azban by.

Azban began to think he would be lying there forever. Then, toward the end of the day, one of the smallest creatures walked by. One of the ants.

Walking right on top of him, he looked down at Azban's flattened-out face and asked, "How can *I* help you? Everyone says that we ants are good for nothing."

Azban had hoped for someone a little bigger than an ant. But he looked up and said, "Oh, no! I think you ants are wonderful. Please go get all of your sisters, brothers, and cousins, and help pull me back into shape. If you do, I promise that I'll always be your friend."

Now, it's not easy being an ant. Other creatures always kicking you around. Not even noticing you. *With a friend as big as Azban,* the ant thought, *maybe everybody will show us a little more respect.*

"I will help," said the ant. "But remember your promise."

"Yes, yes, of course," said Azban. "Now hurry up and get back here with the others."

And so the ant went back to his village.

"Hear me," he said. "Azban the Great has promised he will always be our friend if we help pull him back into shape."

The ants agreed that it would be good to have a friend as big as Azban. And so before long, all of the ants, thousands of them, gathered around the raccoon and began to do something they do very well: work together.

Those ants pulled and pushed and pulled and pushed. They began putting Azban back into shape.

Soon Azban the Raccoon could move. He stood up, and as he did so, he saw that many of the ants were still clinging to his body. Instead of being grateful for what they had done, he just brushed them off and said, "Horrible little ants!"

He began to walk away without even saying thank you.

However, after only a few steps he noticed something. His legs were very short. His body was still quite wide. He had brushed those ants off before they had finished stretching him out.

But having broken his promise, he knew that the ants would never agree to finish the job. Instead, Raccoon had to learn to accept being the short, squatty animal he is to this day.

And he is certainly not a fast runner.